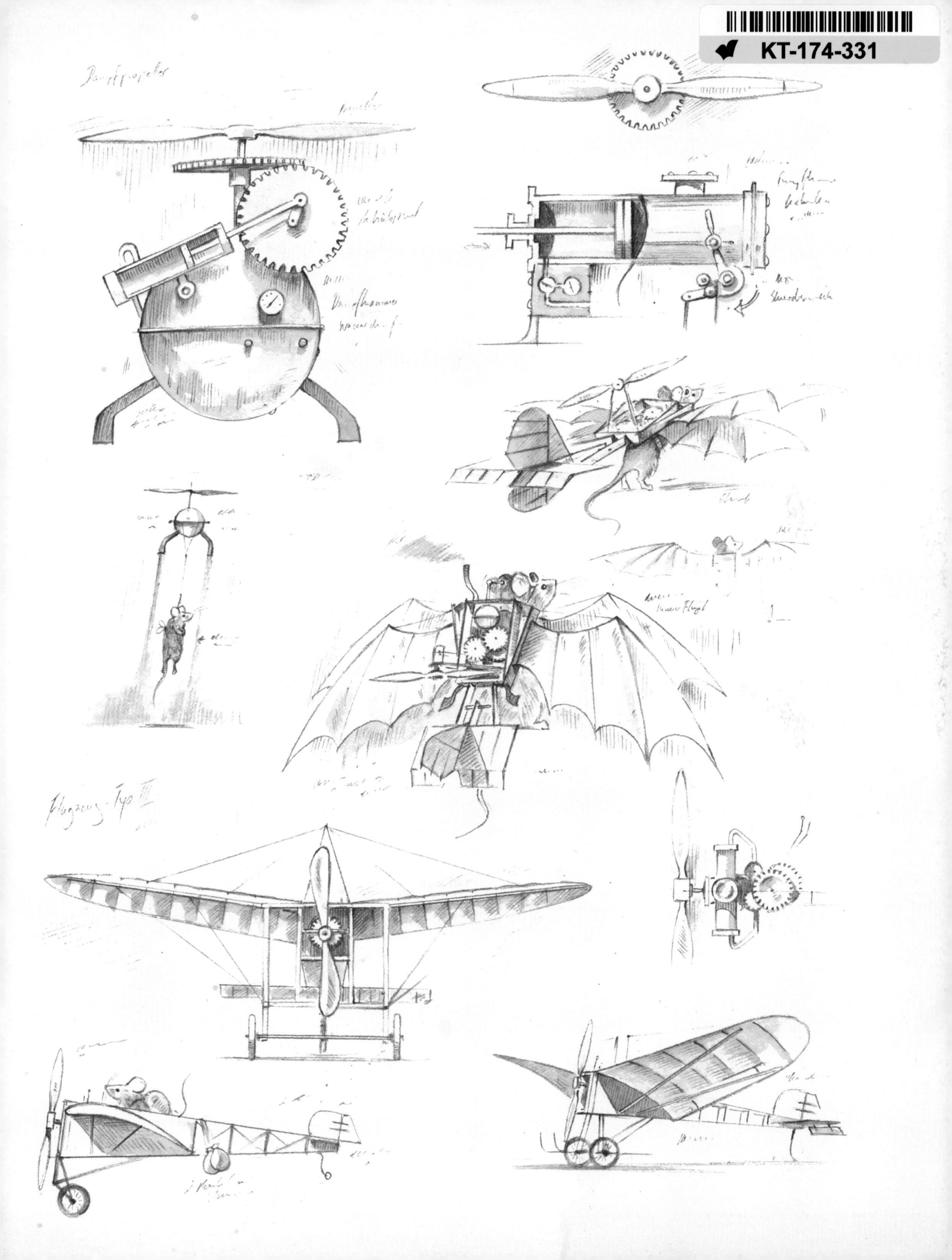

# Foreword

*Lindbergh—The Tale of a Flying Mouse* is a beautifully illustrated story of a little mouse who seeks a new life in America. But how does a mouse leave his home and cross the vast North Atlantic? He flies, of course. What follows is a charming story of a courageous little mouse defying odds to overcome his fears and challenges of the world—avoiding mousetraps, cats, owls, while using his intelligence to solve his problems in a unique way.

As the curator responsible for the caring of Charles Lindbergh's *Spirit of St. Louis* in the Smithsonian Institution's National Air and Space Museum, I thought Lindbergh was inspired to fly the Atlantic nonstop, solo after he read a newspaper account of famed French ace René Fonck's failed attempt in September 1926. Lindbergh, an airmail pilot plying the skies between St. Louis and Chicago, dreamed of bigger things. On his own, he planned his own conquest of the Atlantic, finding financial backers and an aircraft builder willing to design an airplane to his precise specifications. An obscure pilot from the Midwest competing against the greatest names in aviation, Lindbergh triumphed over the same challenges that thwarted his competitors, creating one of the most widely known and transformative stories in American history. And now I know Lindbergh's true inspiration. . . .

*F. Robert van der Linden*
*Chairman*
*Curator of Special Purpose Aircraft*
*Aeronautics Division*
*National Air and Space Museum*
*Smithsonian Institution*

In Loving Memory
of My Father

# LINDBERGH

Special thanks to Aaron Frisch.

First published in the United States, Great Britain, Canada, Australia, and New Zealand in 2014 by NorthSouth Books, Inc., an imprint of NordSüd Verlag AG, CH-8005 Zürich, Switzerland.





Distributed in the United States by NorthSouth Books Inc., New York 10016.
Library of Congress Cataloging-in-Publication Data is available.
ISBN: 978-0-7358-4167-3 (trade edition)
3 5 7 9 • 10 8 6 4 2
Printed in Germany by Offizin Andersen Nexö Leipzig GmbH, 04442 Zwenkau, April 2014.
www.northsouth.com

FSC
www.fsc.org
MIX
Paper from responsible sources
FSC® C012425

Torben Kuhlmann

# LINDBERGH

## The Tale of a Flying Mouse

English Text by Suzanne Levesque

North
South

# A Mouse's Tale

Many years ago in a country across the sea there lived an inquisitive mouse. This little mouse was so curious he would hide away, sometimes for months, to read great books written by humans.

## A Remarkable Disappearance

One day the little mouse returned from his studies, and everything was quiet. Too quiet. The hundreds of mice who once swarmed the city's old haunts to meet friends and gnaw on foods had vanished—seemingly overnight.

It used to be cozy where the humans lived. Their food was rich and abundant, and a mouse could easily snitch a meal from their kitchens—even their dinner plates! The worst thing a greedy mouse could expect was a shriek or a broomstick shooing. But now odd mechanical contraptions were everywhere, and the human world was dangerous. . . .

Hanseanzeiger

Es klappt

William C. Hooker and James Henry Atkinson

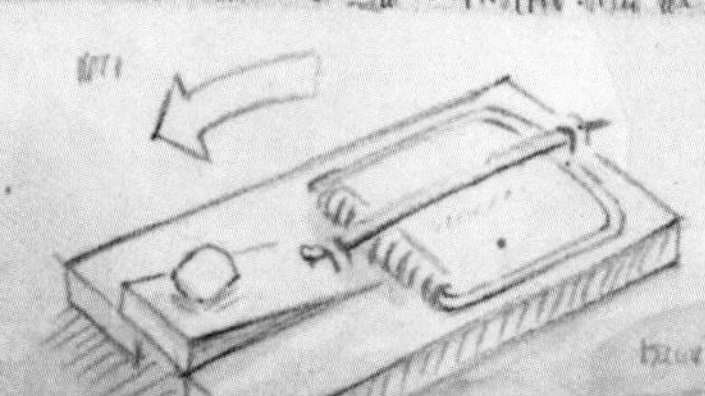

NO MICE

NEW INVENTION

Das sichere Ende d

Mauseplag

## Messages from a Distant Country

Weeks passed with no other mouse to be found. When the little mouse took a look at the newspapers, he suddenly understood—the nightmarish mousetraps were to blame for exiling his friends. But where had they all gone? Maybe America? All the mice knew stories of this faraway place. A huge statue greeted all who arrive there, whether human or mouse.

The little mouse set straight off to the harbor. He would climb aboard a ship like his friends must have done. But now hungry cats guarded the ships like fortresses.

The mouse was lucky to escape down a storm drain. There, it was dark and suddenly very quiet. He felt safe for now.

## Flying Mice?

As he ventured through the maze of sewer tunnels, he sniffed the damp air and heard faint squeaks. Suddenly, wings flapped against his face! Ghostly creatures flew through the dark. They looked like mice, with tiny eyes and huge ears. But they flew with powerful black wings.

The little mouse carefully studied the strange flying relatives

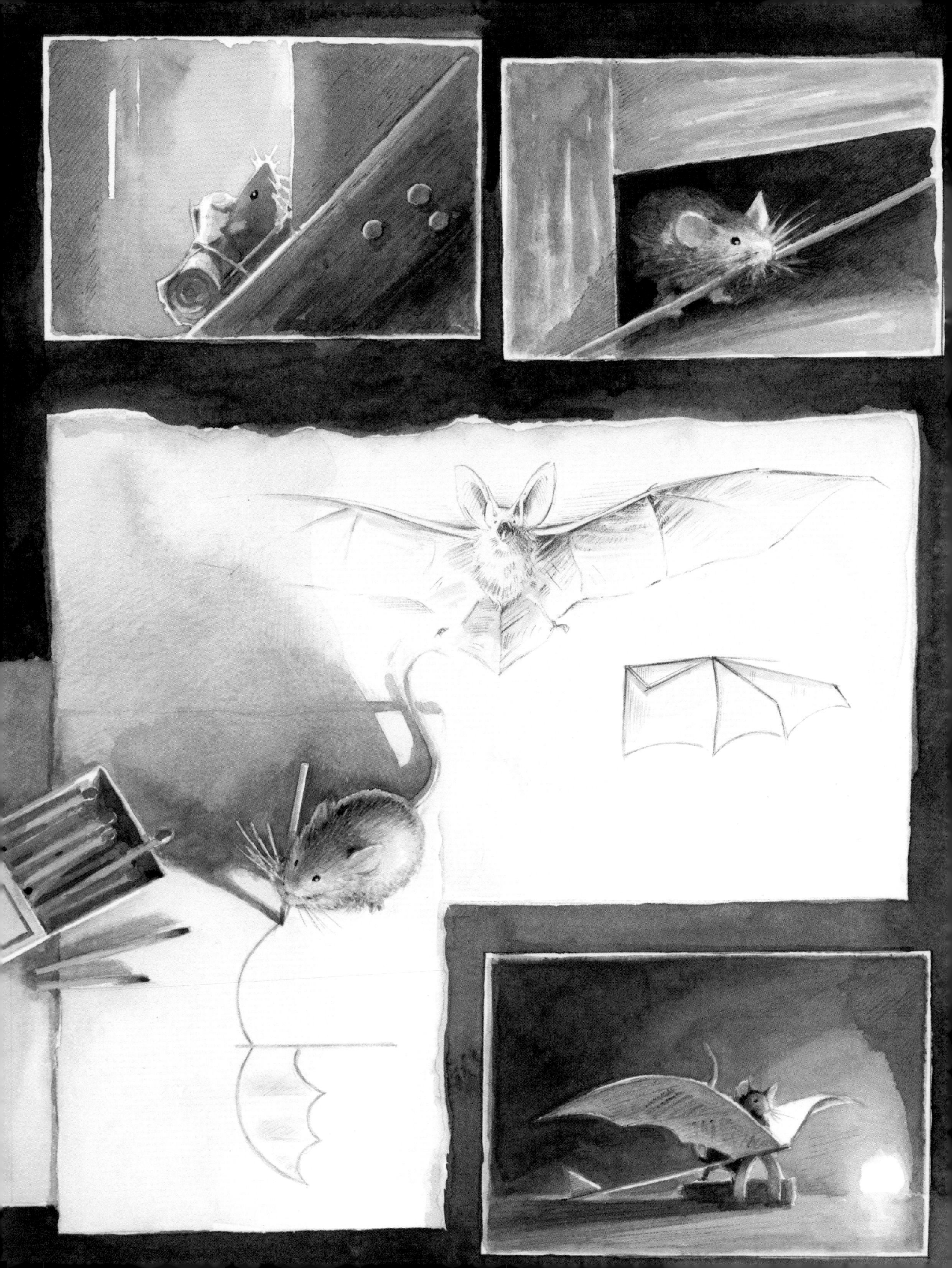

He had an idea! He would find a way to fly, too! How else to reach America? First he collected scraps of wood, shreds of newspaper, string, and glue. Then he began the construction of two large wings and a tiny fin.

At last the mouse decided to test his invention in a vast hall where there were no risky winds—just countless puffing monstrosities collecting swarms of passengers.

Hamburg

The little mouse climbed, leaped . . . and flew! He swung through the air for a moment. But then he tumbled and plunged toward the ground at alarming speed.

*Choochoo!* The small pilot rolled off the tracks only barely avoiding the heavy, crushing wheels.

He sat and looked at the huge steaming machines. Eureka! That was it! Steam! Perhaps that was what his contraption needed. This time his construction was much more complicated. The mouse used many tiny components: gears taken from watches, lighters, small metal housings, and screws. . . .

## A Steam-Powered Flying Mouse

But now the mouse's machine had too much power! It spun and rotated out of control. It needed wings and rudders.

For weeks the clever mouse tinkered with his design. Little by little, a new flying machine grew amid a pile of odds and ends.

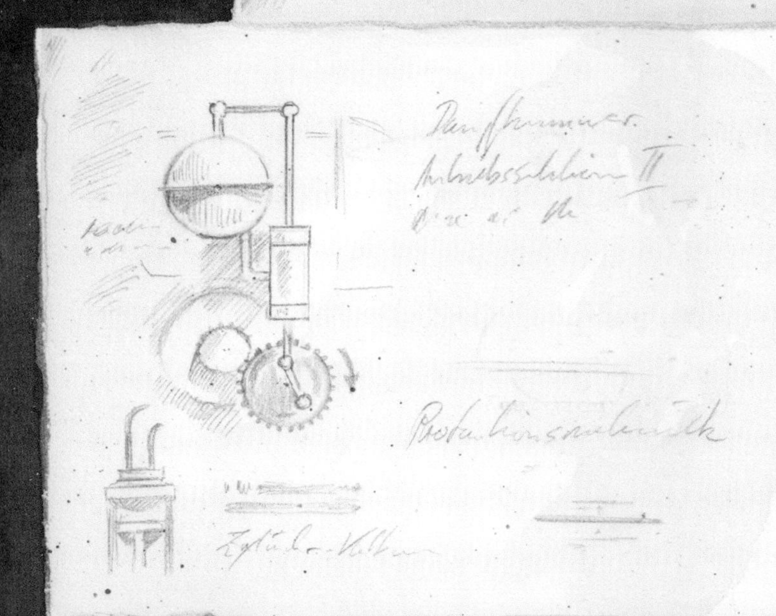

Flieger

This new machine was impressive. A small boiler filled with water produced steam. Pumping pistons moved the cogwheels, and a propeller spun at the end.

Every time the mouse tested the engine, the propeller unleashed a storm and blew away his plans and papers. The tiny inventor was more confident than ever. An actual flight to America seemed within his reach!

DOCK

## Crashed and Discovered!

Unfortunately, the flying machine was now too heavy! When the little aviator sensed he was about to crash, he cut himself free and tumbled to the cobblestones below. He dragged his ruined machine away and went into hiding.

But his secret was out. The next day, pictures of the sky-storming rodent were splashed across all the city's newspapers. "Hamburg's Flying Mouse Spotted!" Everyone wondered what the little daredevil would do next. All eyes were now on the lookout for the winged rodent. Eyes of all kinds . . .

Hamburger Stadtzeitung

SENSATION!

Tollkühne Maus mit Flugapparat

## Flying Boxes and Fierce Persecutors

The little mouse was more determined than ever. He started on a new design with wheels for easier starts and safer landings, broad wings, and a powerful engine. This would be a proper plane, with space for food, supplies, spare parts, and fuel.

Flyer III

Flyer III

Seitenruder

Fahrwerk

Flyer II

But when the mouse ventured out at night to gather parts, he sensed he was being followed. He heard soft whooshes in the dark sky above and saw strange silhouettes on the rooftops. The mysterious figures reappeared night after night, inching closer to the mouse's hideaway.

After a short time the owls began glaring directly at the mouse through the window of his workshop. They took turns keeping watch. And soon the cats began to circle. . . .

## A Secret Escape

The mouse refined his flying masterpiece for weeks, hunting for new materials despite the dangers that lurked around every dark corner. Only the most terrible weather would force his predators to abandon their posts, freeing the roofs and alleys of their watchful eyes.

Then, one foggy, rainy day, the mouse ventured out. His heart was pounding. The owls were still there but were dozing on chimneys. He waded through the empty streets of the city, shrouded by mist as he pulled the heavy aircraft along behind him.

## A Close Call

The little mouse was now soaking wet. He had been creeping through the streets for hours, dodging the solitary figures that occasionally crossed his path—hastily marching people hiding their heads from the rain with newspapers, their leather shoes pounding the wet pavement. Finally, through the fog, the mouse saw the tallest building in the city—the church tower!

It was dark inside. The tower's colossal clock ticked loudly, triggering its tremendous, bellowing chimes to ring every so often. It sent shivers down the little mouse's spine. But by carefully latching on to the clock's constantly rotating gears, he hauled the heavy aircraft to the top of the tower's balcony. Our small mouse could not have asked for a better runway!

The motor started quickly, and the propeller whirred. It was incredibly loud! But that wasn't the only noise. From behind, the mouse heard a rapid, flapping sound!

Owl claws snatched and snapped. The small pilot ducked into his cockpit. With his eyes pinched shut, the mouse yanked at the controls and pulled the wing flaps up as the airplane sped over the edge and . . . flew!

The owls were not far behind. A feisty claw scraped the tail fin of the tiny aircraft. The small aviator pulled the controls sideways, and the flying machine made a steep left turn far too sharp for the owls.

The plane gained altitude and soared up through the clouds. The bell tower, which had seemed so gigantic, was now a mere pin poking through the fog.

## A Skyrocketing Success

Higher and higher he climbed, until he was above the clouds and basking in the rays of the evening sun. The small plane, and its even smaller pilot, flew over fields and cities, past cliffs and lighthouses, until the mighty ocean stretched ahead.

## Over the Atlantic

The little mouse bravely flew on. From time to time he saw a steaming vessel puffing large plumes of smoke and leaving a white foam trail on the surface of the water. These were the same ships the mouse had once wanted to board. Now they chugged toward the distant land and the city with the statue. He need only follow these ships!

Night fell, and the air grew cold. The mouse chewed on a hunk of cheese and tried to ignore his exhaustion while swishing through the dark. After a long night, a new day dawned, and the mouse spotted something far away. . . .

There, behind some clouds, was a huge city!

# NEW YORK

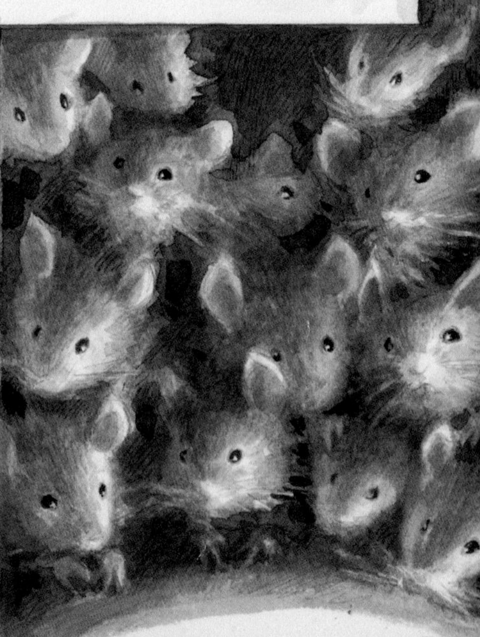

# A Celebrated Arrival

Everything was much larger than the mouse had expected. Houses and towers crowded together, and the tallest buildings scratched the sky with their steel spikes. Thousands of people swarmed through the streets like ants. The mouse spotted the famous statue on a small island. New York! America! He flew toward the harbor and circled over the city. A few passersby looked upward. “Is that a flying mouse?” “It IS a flying mouse!” People stopped walking, and an increasing number of eyes followed the little flying machine.

The excited crowd caught the attention of the city’s mice; some were peeking out of their holes already. The news spread like wildfire, especially through the community of mice. Countless excited gray bundles of fur poured from their hiding places. Our petite pilot geared up for a landing.

As soon as his aircraft settled to a stop, he was surrounded by a sea of scurrying mice.

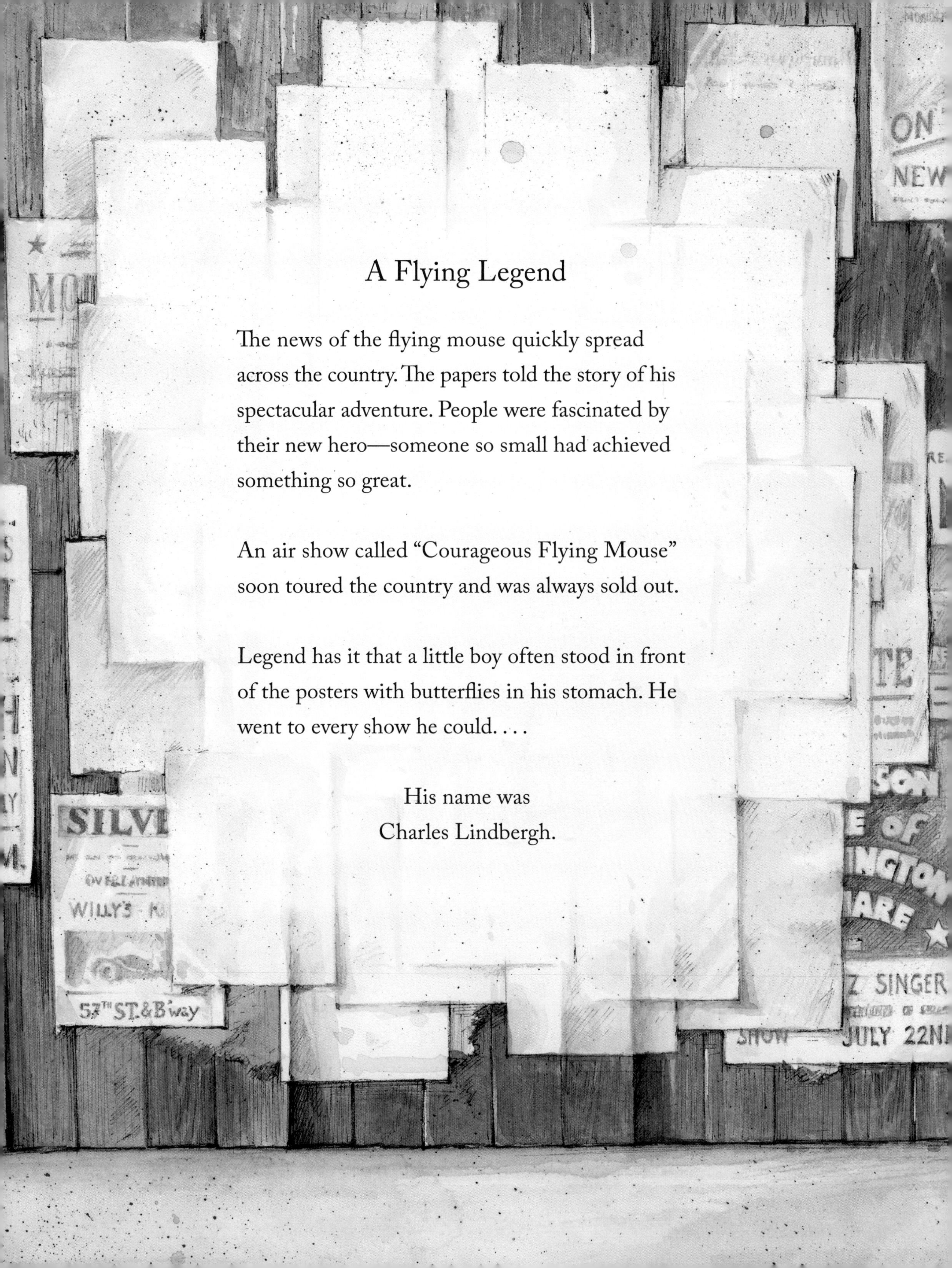


## A Flying Legend

The news of the flying mouse quickly spread across the country. The papers told the story of his spectacular adventure. People were fascinated by their new hero—someone so small had achieved something so great.

An air show called "Courageous Flying Mouse" soon toured the country and was always sold out.

Legend has it that a little boy often stood in front of the posters with butterflies in his stomach. He went to every show he could. . . .

His name was
Charles Lindbergh.

SEPT 10
BOWERY
K, 10TH ST
THE BIG ONE
IMMENSE HIT OF
FOX'S
OLD BOWERY THEATER
NEW DRAMA AND NEW ATTRACTIONS
JOHNNY WILLIAMS
THE PIRATE'S DAUGHTER
CENTRAL PARK
FOURTH WEEK AND STILL CROWDED
MR. G. L. FOX
NEW AIR SHOW
COURAGEOUS
FLYING MOUSE
THE TRANSATLANTIC RODENT HERO
SPECTACULAR
NEW YORK CITY
EVERYDAY 8 P.M.
GREAT ENGLISH THEATERS
A PALPABLE HIT!
COMEDY
TO OVERFLOW
FEATURE
COLLINS
JUNE 3RD
BENEFIT OF MR. N. B. CLARKE
PADDY MI

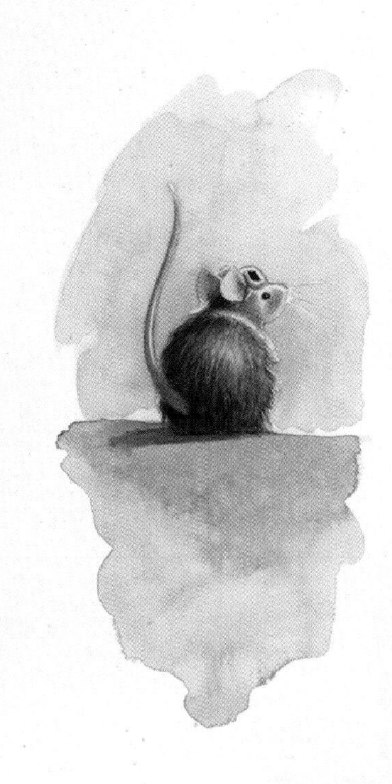

The End

# A short history of aviation

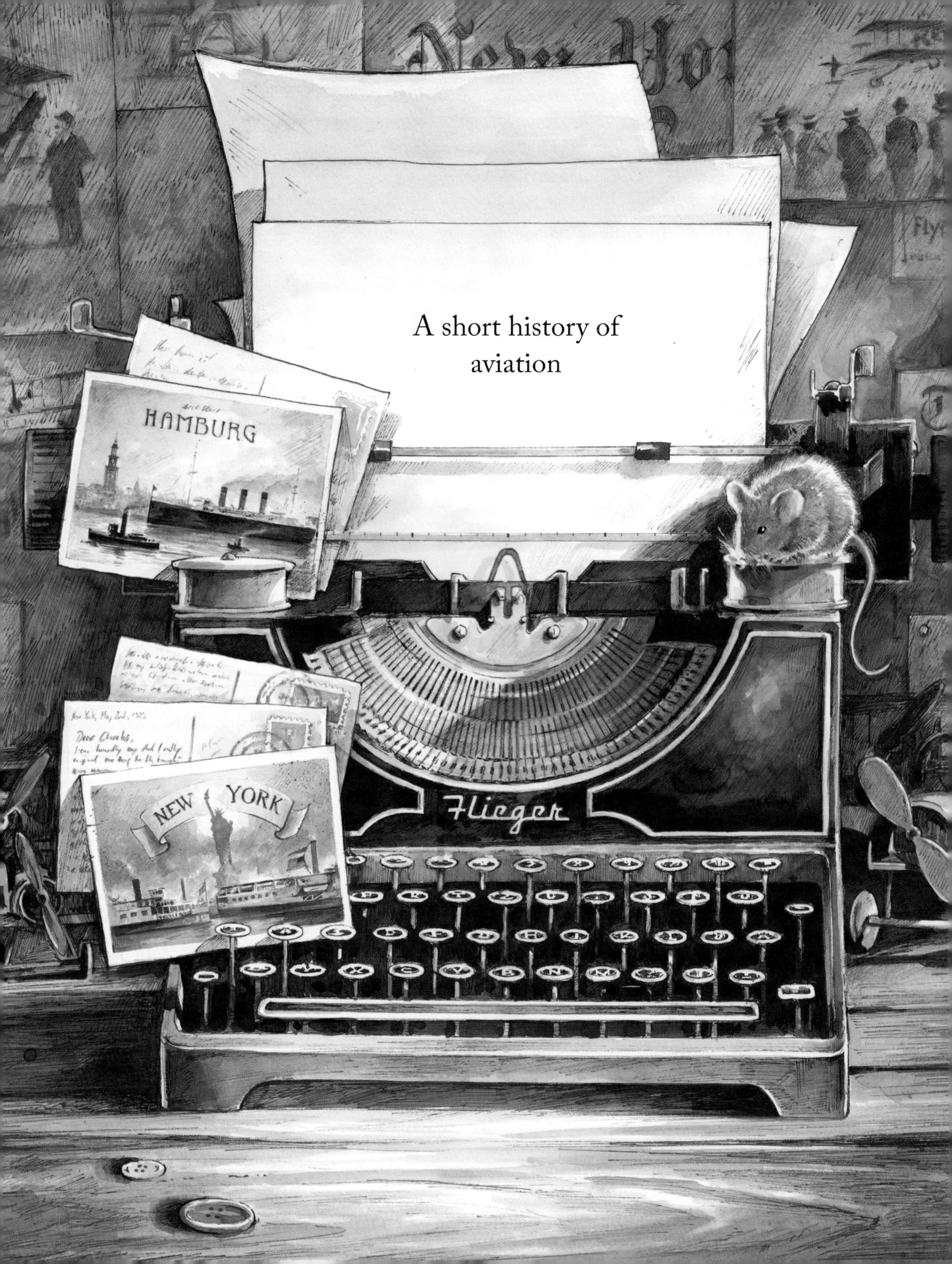

# Otto Lilienthal

German pioneer of aviation Otto Lilienthal was the originator of the hang glider. With his construction, he made many successful flights. Sadly, his last flight on August 9, 1896, cost him his life.

# The Wright Brothers

The American brothers Wilbur and Orville Wright transformed the idea of travel. The biplane construction *Flyer* made its first ascent into the sky on December 17, 1903. Their flight lasted a mere twelve seconds.

*Spirit of St. Louis*

# Charles Lindbergh

Charles Augustus Lindbergh Jr. was an American pilot and a pioneer in the history of aviation. In 1927 he crossed the Atlantic Ocean without a stopover in his single-engine aircraft *Spirit of St. Louis*. He was the first pilot to achieve this single-handedly.

Lindbergh started early in the morning on May 20 in New York City. To keep the plane as light as possible, Lindbergh flew without a radio or a parachute! Roughly 33 hours later and after a 3,600-miles-long flight he landed in Paris. On his adventurous journey, he was confronted with a snowstorm and challenged by his growing exhaustion.

After his successful flight over the Atlantic Ocean, Lindbergh returned to the United States as a true-blue hero and was known as a legend of aviation ever since.

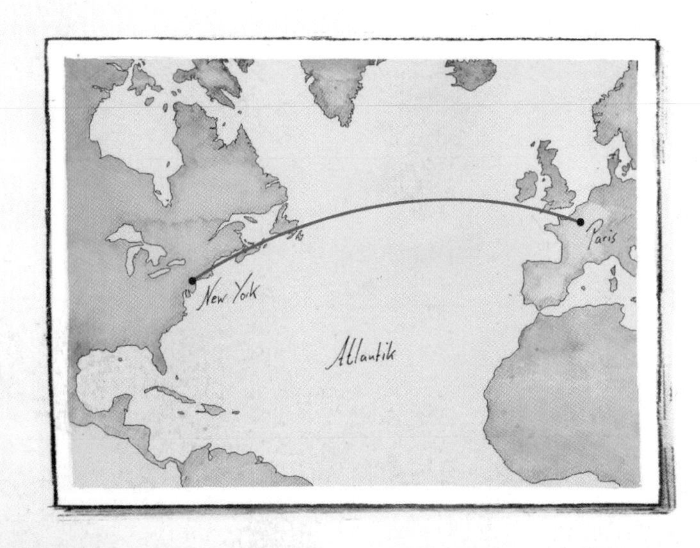


*Lindbergh's flight path across the Atlantic*

N-X-211

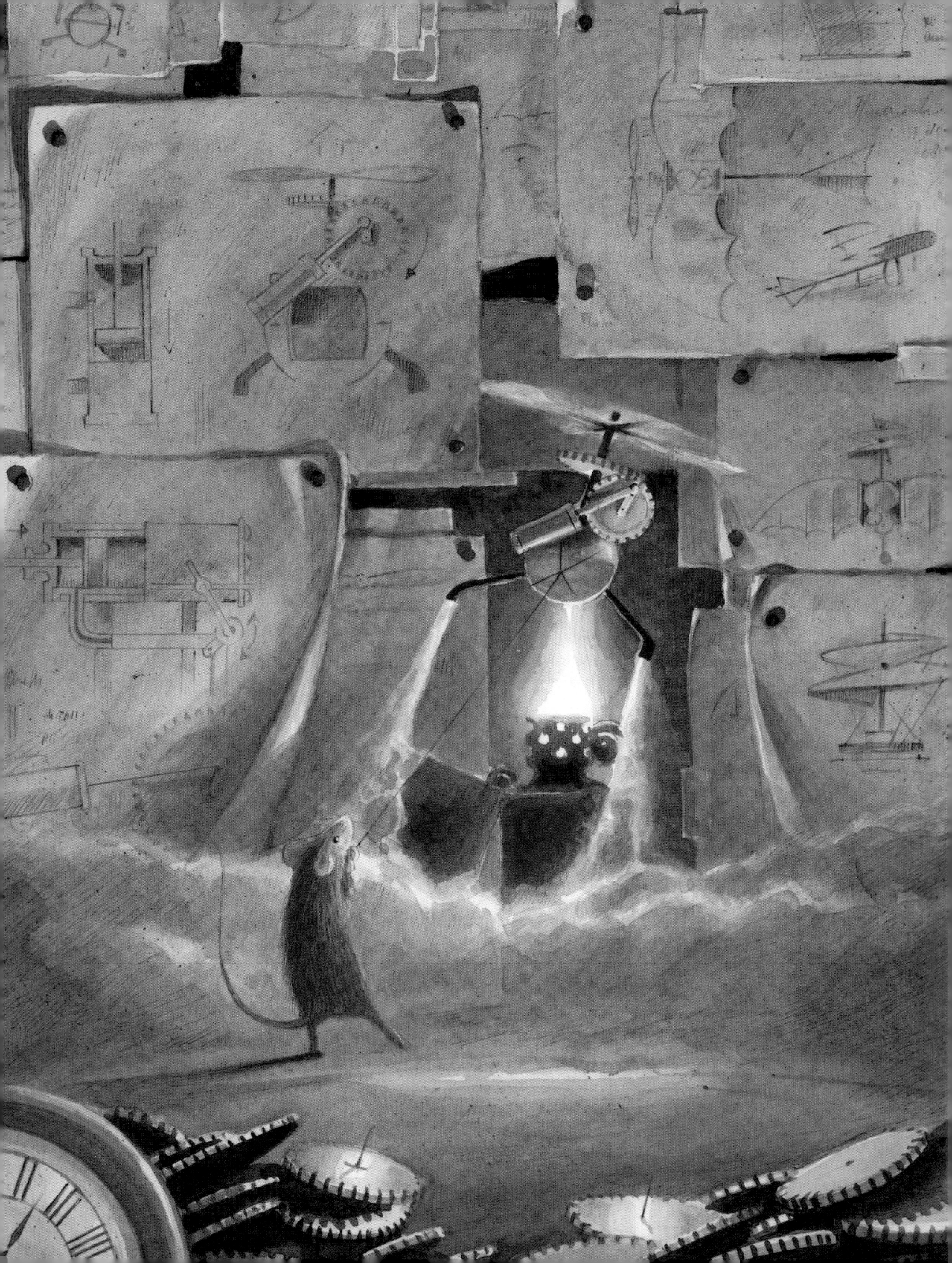

# Torben Kuhlmann

Torben Kuhlmann studied illustration and communication design at the HAW Hamburg, in Germany, with a concentration in book illustration. In June 2012 he graduated having completed the children's book *Lindbergh—The Tale of a Flying Mouse*. *Lindbergh* is Torben Kuhlmann's first illustrated book. It shows his enthusiasm for peculiar inventions and his interest in the colorful history of aviation. Since childhood he has expressed a keen interest in building small mechanical contraptions. One might say Kuhlmann has a similar demeanor to our hero in *Lindbergh*!

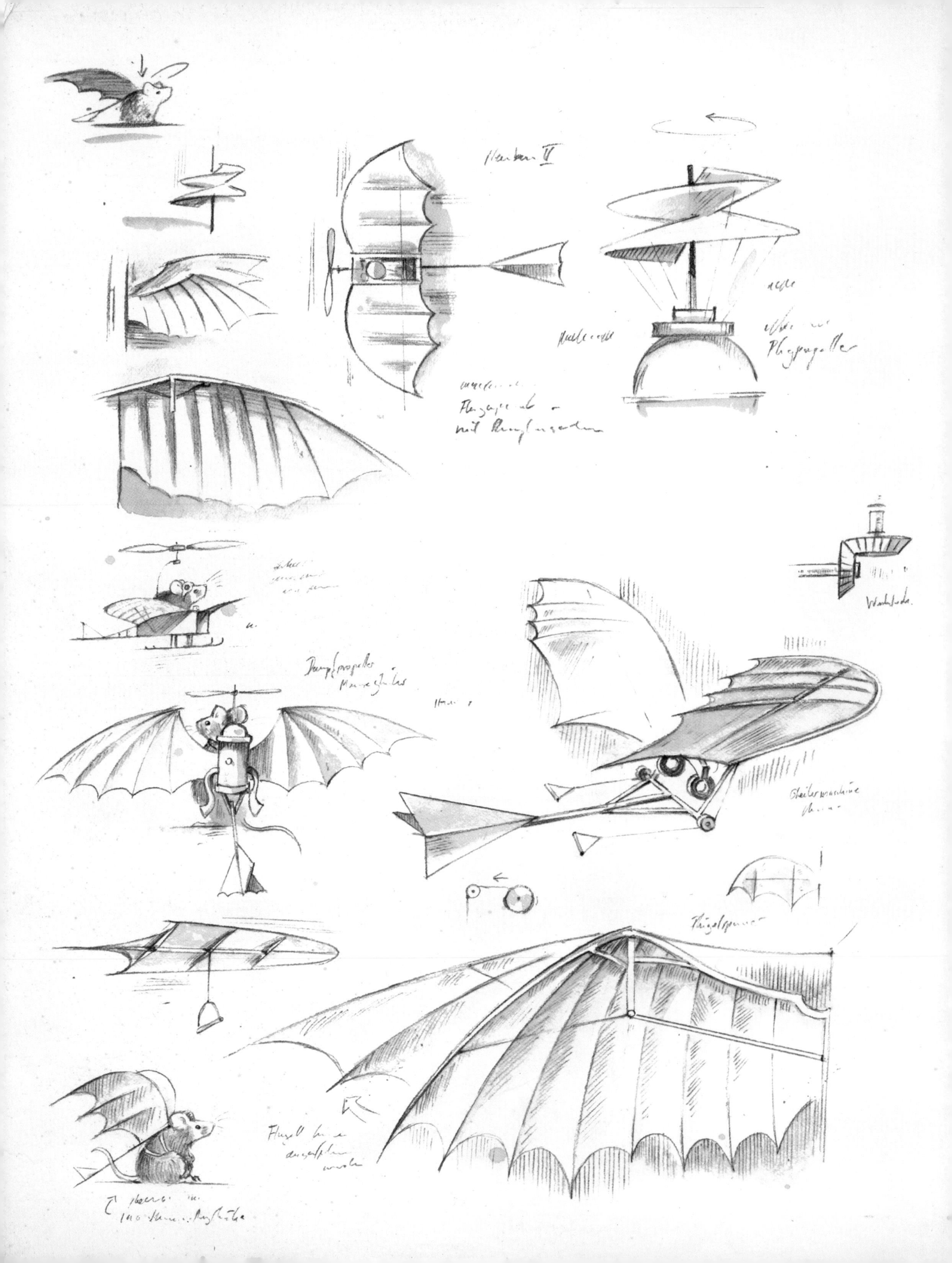